CW00972107

LITTLE BILLY BUCKET

LYNDSAY THWAITES

ANDRE DEUTSCH

On *Monday* Little Billy was playing First Bear on the Moon. He found some macaroni tins and he put them on his feet for moon boots. It was a great game. But . . .

"Look, Mum, look, I'm stuck!" he said. Mrs Bucket was
very busy with some wallpaper.
"I can't stop now, dear," she said, without looking, "but I
can see you're having a good time exploring!"
Mrs Bucket had her mind on other things.

On *Tuesday* Little Billy was playing Funny Clowns at the Circus. He found an old tub and he jumped right into it. It was a great game. But . . .

"Look, Mum, look, I'm stuck!" he said. Mrs Bucket was
very busy. She was standing on the table.
"I can't stop now, dear," she called, without looking, "but
I can see you're having a good time bouncing!"
Mrs Bucket had her mind on other things.

On *Wednesday* Little Billy was playing Knights in Armour.
He found an old Weetie box and he made holes for his
head and arms. It was a great game. But . . .

"Look, Mum, look, I'm stuck!" he said. Mrs Bucket was
very busy holding up the wallpaper.
"I can't stop now, dear," she cried without looking, "but I
can see you're having a good time galloping!"
Mrs Bucket had her mind on other things.

On *Thursday* Little Billy was playing Robots of the Future. He found two 'thingummys' and he pushed his arms right into them. It was a great game. But . . .

"Look, Mum, look, I'm stuck!" he said. Mrs Bucket was
very busy mopping up some spilt paste.
"I can't stop now, dear," she muttered without looking,
"but I can see you're having a good time marching!"
Mrs Bucket had her mind on other things.

On *Friday* Little Billy was playing Billy Bucket's Fudge Factory. He mixed some flour, spice and honey in a big pot. It looked just like fudge and Little Billy ate it all – then he licked out the pot. But . . .

"Where are you, Mum, I'm stuck!" he said. Mrs Bucket
was very busy painting fine lines.
"I can't stop now, dear," she gasped, without looking,
"but I can see you're having a good time in the kitchen!"
Mrs Bucket had her mind on other things.

On *Saturday* Mrs Bucket put down her paints and brushes. "I've finished at last," she said. "Now where's my Little Billy?"

When Mrs Bucket saw him she nearly fainted.

"Oh, my poor little Billy!" she cried, "whatever have you done?"

She put him in a buggy and ran to Doctor Bunting's house. "Doctor, Doctor," Mrs Bucket cried, "Look at my poor little Billy!"

Doctor Bunting looked. Then he laughed and laughed.
"Don't worry, Mrs Bucket," he said. "We'll have him out
in a jiffy."

Doctor Bunting went to his cupboard and took out a big green bottle. The label on the bottle said Super Slippery Stuff.

"I'll need your help, Mrs Bucket," said Doctor Bunting.

They turned Little Billy Bucket upside down. Then Doctor Bunting tipped the Super Slippery Stuff all down the inside and all over the outside of the things stuck on Little Billy. Little Billy became super slippery and Doctor Bunting was able to pull off . . .

Monday's macaroni tins,
Tuesday's tub,
Wednesday's Weetie box,
Thursday's 'thingummys',
Friday's fudge pot.

Then Little Billy Bucket stood before them damp and dripping. "My Little Billy is unstuck!" cried Mrs Bucket, full of joy. "Speak to me, my little boy!"
But Little Billy just said "YUK!"

Mrs Bucket rubbed Little Billy's fur clean and dry with a big towel. "I've been so busy," she said, hugging him, "I haven't been fair – I just didn't notice my own little Bear."

Then Mrs Bucket said, "Now let me think! Let's tidy up today – then tomorrow I'll make your favourite cake, my best honey tarts, and a raspberry drink. And then, I tell you what – we'll go and find a picnic spot." Mrs Bucket hurried off humming, to get everything ready.

"Before you go, Little Billy," said Doctor Bunting, "what are you going to do with all this junk on my floor?"
Little Billy looked at the things that had been stuck on him for so long. "They're not *junk*," he said, "They could be useful."
He took them out into the garden and was very busy for quite a while.
Then – "Come and see," called Little Billy.

"Look . . . Monday's macaroni tins for the birds.

Tuesday's tub for your geraniums.

Wednesday's Weetie box for your cats.

Thursday's thingummys for the water butt

and Friday's fudge pot for your hens."
"Well, thank you, Billy Bucket," said Doctor Bunting with a surprised smile. "You are a brainy little bear full of bright ideas!"

The next day was a fine *Sunday*. Little Billy and Mrs Bucket invited Doctor Bunting to come on their picnic. They set off early and had a lovely day together.

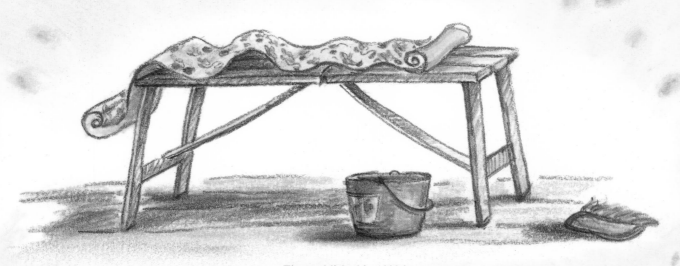

First published in 1989 by
André Deutsch Limited
105–106 Great Russell Street, London WC1B 3LJ

Copyright © 1989 by Lyndsay Thwaites
All Rights reserved

British Library Cataloguing in Publication Data

Thawaites, Lyndsay
Little Billy Bucket.
I. Title
823′.914 [J]

ISBN 0-233-98447-X

Typeset by AKM Associates (UK) Ltd
Ajmal House, Hayes Road, Southall, London
Printed in Great Britain by Cambus Litho Ltd